Guardian

A Journey to the Heart

OTHER BOOKS BY MATT RAWLINS

The Green Bench

The Green Bench II

The Lottery

There's an Elephant in the Room

Emails from Hell

The Container

The Question

The Namer

Mysteries Beyond the Gate

Rediscovering Reverence, The Path to Intimacy

Books can be ordered through bookstores or
Amazon.

Ebooks are available for $5.99 at:
mrawlinsonline.com.

Guardian
A Journey to the Heart

Matt Rawlins

Amuzement Publications

Guardian by Matt Rawlins.
Copyright © 2011 Matt Rawlins.

Feel free to contact Matt if you have any questions at: mrawlins@mac.com

Cover designer - Thank you, Kelvin Marc Tan.

Editor: Thank you, Aimee Rawlins

Watch over your heart with all diligence, For from it flow the springs of life.
Proverbs 4:23

Welcome

Welcome my Friend.

Come, sit and relax.
Rest your weary soul.
You have traveled far.
But I fear distance is not the mark of a journey,
At least not this journey.

This journey is a very short distance, strictly
speaking.
It is the distance from the head to the heart.

But the gap between these two has:
Torn nations apart,
Split families,
Divided friends,
Crushed personalities,
And broken the heart of God.

It is not for the weak or fearful,
But it is a journey worth taking.
It may be the only journey worth taking,
But I will leave that assessment to you.

Prologue

A journey was birthed in the heart of God.

The journey is God's idea.
It started in his heart,
As all true journeys do.

God thought of life as he loved it,

The raw power of creating stars and galaxies.

He remembered the joy of intimacy in all eternity past.

He gathered his favorite stories and how love was expressed.

He then carefully took the essence of all those memories,

And placed them in a longing.

It included the triumphant joy of power,
An aching honesty for the truth,
Courage for authenticity,
And a tender wooing for intimacy.

Then all heaven watched in utter amazement
As God humbled himself and went to a small galaxy,
And then in more humility, to a very small planet.
He took a pinch of dust from the planet and formed
a shell for this longing to dwell in.

He then gathered this longing and held it in a single
breath.

Carefully, oh so slowly, so as not to scatter or destroy
the dust,

He breathed the longing into it.

His life,

His desires,

His joys and all that was worth celebrating,

Now dwelt in this dust man.

Chapter 1

Now, my friend, as you read this, we have so few
words to describe this next season of time and the
relationship of God to this dust man.

I will only give you a glimpse, as on a foggy day, or
through a darkened mirror, of this glorious life and
why we suffer so much today.

The dust man stood with his eyes closed.
Before he could open his eyes and focus them,
Before his mind framed words to engage the world,
Just at the first beat of his heart,

He experienced it.

He gasped.

He moaned.

Then groaned.

A rumbling laughter broke out of him as he
unconsciously raised his arms.

Finally, he yelled out in ecstasy at the top of his voice.

The first sound heard on the dust planet was pure, raw delight.

His eyes began to water.

He licked his lips to see if it was a taste.

He slowly moved his body to see if it was something that was on him.

As he moved, his body came alive.

He could feel the blood flowing through his veins. His heart found its beat and, with it, rhythm.

His lungs filled with sweet, rich air. He took a deep breath, and then quickly gave it back.

Electric stimuli broke out all over his body as his muscles moved. He slowly moved his fingers, then wrists, then arms and continued to explore. The movement of his muscles was brilliant.

As his muscles moved, he became aware of his bones and joints. He twisted them and felt the joints move against each other, the tendons holding tight and yet yielding to each other.

He felt it all. Each twitch, response, movement or signal. The breath was so much more than his body, yet his body was soaking it all in.

These emotions surged through every part of him as the breath began to ease up. Just before he was sure he could take no more and would burst, it stopped.

His first conscious thought was, *I will spend my whole life trying to explain, discover, celebrate and understand that feeling I felt rushing into me.*

The dust man opened his eyes, and slowly they began to focus. He looked around the garden he was in and was stunned at the beauty around him. In one moment, it all disappeared before him. At this moment, there are no words to describe what he saw. Let us just simply say that he saw God.

The dust man smiled, and as his eyes focused, he saw the source of the breath. Like a newborn child put on its mothers breast, once again hearing that familiar heart beat, the dust man found his Creator and rested in him.

Chapter 2

As the dust man continued his work in the garden, he had a growing sense that he could not explain. It was like nothing he had experienced. There was an ache inside of him. He found himself walking long distances in the garden and looking at the animals and life around him, but each step he sensed he had not found it yet. Whatever it was.

The ache within him grew stronger and more intense. On such days, he would run for miles through the soft grass and fields. Finally, he would have to stop, exhausted and momentarily distracted from his search.

On one day, God was with Adam (for that was the dust man's given name) in the garden, and they were enjoying each other's presence. The ache within him grew so intense he began to weep. It wasn't pain as we would understand it; it was longing. Adam imagined if his body was alive before the Breath, it must have felt this, only much more intensely. It was an invitation. It was almost as if his body was calling out, summoning help.

At that moment, Adam turned to look to his Creator and saw a beaming smile come across his face. Anticipation grew in Adam, and as it grew, he fell into a deep sleep.

Adam woke up and lay on the grass for a moment. Remembering the smile on God's face, he looked towards him and saw another person with him. And with an encouragement Adam and Eve felt from God, they turned their attention on each other.

They walked slowly towards each other. They finally stood face to face, nose to nose, their foreheads touching. Eyes closed and their breath was in the same space. They stood completely vulnerable, together, and just were.

The journey grew richer with this new expression.

Chapter 3

Adam walked towards what he knew would be the familiar sound of God walking in the garden. As always, Adam felt him coming before he heard or saw him.

A renewed sense of the first breath followed. He stood and allowed the experience to intensify in him again. It was now richer, more subtle and refined than the first raw experience. Like iron ore drawn to a magnet, everything in him awoke as he heard and then finally saw God walking towards him.

Adam stood quietly in the presence of God. Neither was in a hurry to move on or say anything. It was their moment of unspeakable intimacy, and words would only be a distraction. How long this took, we shall never know, for in their world a day is like a thousand years in ours.

As they were together, a new experience awoke in Adam. His hands closed gently into fists. He slowly slid his feet apart and separated them to get his balance. He sensed his legs slowly bending just a bit to lower his center of gravity. He slowed his breath, and his eyes darted around as if searching for something. It felt natural but totally new to him.

Adam spoke, "I am not sure what this is, but I am more aware. The word I would use I think is 'ready,' but I am not sure for what?"

A word grew in his mind, and he finally spoke the word out, "Guardian. I am a guardian. But I don't know of what, Father."

"It is my most precious gift of all. I value this above all other gifts I have given to you," God stated.

The man took a step back and took a deep breath. "You value this gift above all the others?" Adam asked.

God smiled and said, "It is the most precious one, as it is a choice to protect everything else I have given to you."

Adam thought for a few moments and then asked, "Is being a guardian the same thing as having a free choice?"

"In a sense, yes. A choice is the raw capacity you have, but to help direct, guide and be responsible with this capacity, I have woven into your choice the desire and position to be a guardian of beauty, wisdom, truth, joy and life. You are to guard that which is valuable and thus worthy of these things," God responded.

Adam stood for a time in the presence and let the words find their place in him. Finally, he spoke out, "Are you saying I am to use my choice to guard myself?"

God gave assurance to Adam that, yes, it was his desire for Adam.

"But you are my guard. You protect me. You watch over me. Your eyes are always on me. That is my greatest joy," Adam declared.

"Yes, and it shall always be that way. I will guard you from the outside. I will take care of those things that are bigger than you. But you must use your choice to guard your own heart. You, and you alone, can do that, for it is yours."

Adam turned his head slowly to face God as a revelation grew in him, "For You. For you alone are worthy. You are what I am to guard, and since you have given yourself to me, I am to guard you in me. I am to guard myself in you. I get it, I don't know from what, but I will guard you, me, us, with my very life."

"Yes, that is a good way to say it," God replied, "For what I have given to you is very valuable, my life and now also your life. Your primary role is to guard over it and protect it from everything but me."

They were together for a day or so longer. Adam moved on to continue his role taking care of the garden. As he walked away, he slowly drew his hands into fists and looked around him saying, "I am a Guardian. I will guard life and all that is precious to him in me."

Chapter 4

"Father, I have found nothing to guard myself from. Everything you have made is wonderful to me," Adam stated as he was with God one day.

As they walked along, they slowed and stood before a beautiful fruit tree, "Yes, I can see that. For that reason I have placed this tree here. You are to guard yourself by not eating the fruit of this tree."

"I must not eat of this tree? I am to guard myself from it, but I can eat the fruit of any other tree?" Adam asked.

"Yes, any other tree is yours to enjoy. This tree you are not allowed to eat from. This will teach you the power of your choice. It will show you the art of defense and protection. Begin now with this tree, and there will be other opportunities to come. But know this clearly, if you eat of it, you will certainly be separated from me, and that will be your death," God responded.

"The tree is my enemy then. I must guard myself from its evil," Adam declared.

"The tree is simply a tree. The power of good and evil is in the choice you have to choose me over this tree. The tree will only reveal who you are and give you an opportunity to grow up in our relationship if you choose to."

"I must confess, Father, that I don't really understand what you are saying, but I trust you. I will guard, defend and protect myself from this tree," Adam stated as he turned away from the tree to tell Eve of this.

Chapter 5

"How can a tree that is deeply rooted in the ground, that cannot move, be an enemy to us?" Adam asked Eve.

"I'm not sure. It seems simple enough to defend ourselves from it, as we just don't touch it or go near it, and we are safe," Eve replied.

"I must think more about this as it baffles me in ways I cannot describe. I think I will go for a run and ponder it for a while," Adam stated as he moved off to enjoy the challenge of a long run.

* * *

Adam returned from his long run, spent both mentally and physically. He could not understand how, if he was to guard himself from the tree, it could not be evil. He walked to the tree and saw a new animal talking with Eve. He was always fascinated with the animals and loved to watch them to figure out what they were before he greeted them and named them. He listened to the conversation.

The animal asked Eve, "Did God really say, 'You shall not eat fruit from any tree in the garden'?"[1]

Eve replied, "From the fruit of the trees of the garden we may eat, but God did say, from the fruit of the tree which is in the middle of the garden, you shall not eat from it or touch it, or you will die."

"You surely will not die," the animal said to the woman. "For God knows that in the day you eat from it, your eyes will be opened, and you will be like God, knowing good and evil."

The world around Adam began to spin. The conversation replayed itself in his mind. He could see the possibility of different choices ahead of Eve. She could be influenced by others to move towards the tree and take its fruit.

She could be influenced to guard anything.

That was the power within her.

That was the power within him.

The tree didn't have to move, it was our choices, our heart that moved us. The power was within us. Such raw power was theirs. Adam looked around quickly to see where God was and he was nowhere to be seen. God would not stop them.

It was their choice.

Adam watched in amazement as Eve moved towards the tree. He could tell she looked at it differently. She reached up and ever so cautiously touched the fruit and then withdrew her hand quickly.

She turned to look directly at Adam, who stood absolutely still as they stared at each other.

Eve reached up and pulled a fruit off the tree and held it in her hand. She looked it over carefully.

After a few moments, she then began to look around to see if anyone else was watching. Slowly she put the fruit to her mouth and took a bite.

Adam gasped and then just stared at her.

His body finally gave out on him as he fell to the ground.

No words could be spoken; they would not fit or describe what had just happened. The weight of his own choice grew before him.

What would he choose to do now?

What should he guard?

The pain of the choice grew more intense within him. Eve, his intimate one--Adam reached down and touched his ribs--she was formed from a rib taken from his own body, she was so much of his life. He took a deep breath, which changed the focus of his thinking immediately. God had put his breath within Adam. The Almighty God had given himself to him. Adam had promised, given his word, that he would guard himself for God alone. Oh how he loved God, the joy of his presence and being with him.

Eve walked swiftly over to Adam and sat down next to him. She held the fruit up to him, offering it to him.

He stared into her eyes and held them. He could feel the innocence draining from her. He could sense something new in her. It was bittersweet, almost hard, while inviting and yet defiant. She was willing to push him away at any suggestion that he didn't agree with her.

She needed him now more than ever. Before he could stop himself, he reached up and took of the fruit and bit into it.

The guardian is now guilty and alienated from the source of life.

Chapter 6

Adam, the guardian, felt it.

He was Exposed.

Vulnerable.

Uncovered.

Laid bare.

A chill ran through his body as he realized he was all on his own.

He realized that he had taken so much for granted up until this moment.

He had lost the joy of his innocence. It was not a part of his physical life as he had assumed. It was the fruit of his choices.

He had lost the confidence of purity. It was not woven into his being as he had thought; it was there because he had guarded his heart for the purposes in which he was made.

He had lost the thrill of abandoning himself to vulnerability. The vulnerability was not forced on him and never had been. He had been giving himself to God and Eve in each moment as an expression of God in him. It was there because he had chosen it.

The wonder of his choices in the past amazed him. The power he had held in his hands that had produced the life he so loved was not only a gift from God, it was the fruit of his choices. He was what he was because he had guarded his heart.

A new awareness grew in him. He was what he was now as a result of that same power in him. New feelings awoke in him.

Guilt replaced innocence. He had not fulfilled his responsibility to guard his heart. He had chosen his own selfish desire for Eve over God's far greater worth.

Shame replaced purity. He was not worthy and would cause a loss of respect to his Father. He would break his Father's heart.

The weight of his choice grew heavier and heavier to the point of overwhelming agony. The realization that Eve might see him in this condition awoke. It was as if his nakedness stood for everything they had enjoyed before, now gone.

He turned to look at Eve, and in that moment they both knew everything had changed. They were both naked, vulnerable, exposed. They could see the same look of sheer terror in each other's eyes. No words were needed. No words could even begin to express what was going on at that moment. There were things to do.

Their greatest gift automatically kicked in. They found some large fig leaves and gathered some vines and sewed them together to cover themselves from the emotions they felt as they looked at their naked bodies.

Adam felt God coming. His body's first response was to run to his Father. But then he looked at the fig leaves covering his body. Guilt and shame seemed to overwhelm him. He knew they would not protect him. He looked around and saw a large tree a short distance away and ran for it. He cowered behind it.

"Where are you?" God finally called out.[1]

"I heard you coming, and I was afraid because I am naked. So I hid," Adam responded.

"Who told you that you were naked?"

Silence.

"Have you not guarded your heart as I told you to and eaten from the tree?" God asked.

Adam rose from behind the tree and was silent for a moment. The guilt and shame pressing hard on him, finally he stated, "The woman YOU put here with me--she gave me some of the fruit and I ate it."

God then asked the woman, "What is this you have done?"

Eve crawled out from under a bush and pointed at the animal that had talked with her and stated, "That animal, the serpent deceived me, and I ate."

Chapter 7

You may have passed over a key point in the last chapter too quickly I fear. It is easy to do, in such a familiar story.

Adam, the guardian, used his gift to protect himself from God.

What God had given to him, such a precious and vulnerable gift, to protect his own heart and thus his relationship with God, was now used against God.

The beloved Adam, who had enjoyed the presence of his Creator and found his abode with him for days on end, now turned on God and attacked him by blaming him for being the source of the problem. ("The woman YOU gave to me.")

The question might sound like this:
What could possibly cause a man who is deeply in love for such a long time, in one moment to turn and blame his beloved as the one who is at fault for what he has done?

It is the gift at work. Remember, it truly is a wonderful gift, given at great cost to a vulnerable God. *We are guardians.* We were to guard that which was most precious to us, that which was truly worthy. That was meant to be our relationship with God, but then Adam let down his guard. One very foolish and rebellious choice.

Now what does he guard?

He chooses to guard his own heart from anything that would make him feel vulnerable, exposed, weak or needy.

His greatest enemy now appears to him to be God.

It is his choice. He has the bold audacity, backed by his shame and guilt, to stand before heaven and declare the Vulnerable One as the source of the problem.

In reality, this most precious gift is now the problem.

Chapter 8

You might say that seems a bit strong to say. The gift is now the problem. Maybe you are willing to admit it is "a" problem at times, but to make such a bold statement must be an exaggeration.

History teaches us the answer if we will look.

Adam and Eve are removed from the garden, and the very next story is about their two sons, Cain and Abel.

Abel takes care of flocks, and Cain works in the field. They both bring the fruit of their toil to God as an offering, and God favors Abel's offering over Cain's.

Cain goes away angry and hurt.

At what you ask?

His brother's offering exposes his inadequate gift that God does not accept. He feels vulnerable and exposed.

God sees Cain's response and says to him, "Why are you angry? Why are you discouraged? If you do what is right, I will accept you, won't I? But if you are not willing to be vulnerable to me, be aware, sin is crouching at the door, but you must protect our relationship. It is your choice."

Cain makes his decision and invites his brother for a walk in a field. He then kills him. Cain would rather destroy his brother than expose his own inadequacy. Rather than be vulnerable and confess his need for help, he lets the jealousy of his own heart take action. He will kill to guard his heart.

Generations are born, and soon man's heart is so corrupt that every inclination of the thoughts of his heart is only towards evil all the time.

Humanity will not deal with its heart. We will do anything to give it the pleasure we want or to destroy anything that would make us feel vulnerable, which as a general rule is everyone else.

God sends a flood to destroy the whole earth, and only Noah and his family are saved.

We see the first civilization after the flood. What is their response? They join together and declare, "Let us build ourselves a city, with a tower that reaches to the sky and build a name for ourselves."

Why do they need a tower that rises to the sky? They now need to protect themselves from God, who can destroy them with a flood. A society is born that seeks to be in complete control of life. They will create a nation that will play the role of Guardian and replace the need for a God to protect us from the elements.

We are only 11 chapters into the story of mankind. Still not convinced?

Job will condemn God in order to try and justify himself.

Abraham will give his wife (his inheritance) away to protect himself.

Cunning Jacob will betray his brother to steal his birthright and protect himself.

The sons of Jacob will sell Joseph, their brother, to deal with the pain he causes them with his dreams and apparent self-exaltation.

Saul will throw a spear at a young commander in his army (David) and try to destroy him to protect himself.

David, a man after God's own heart, will commit adultery and then kill the woman's husband to protect himself.

Jeroboam, a king, will build two golden calves and call them God in order to protect his kingdom. It will keep the Israelites from going to Jerusalem to offer sacrifices as God commanded.

Soon they will offer up their children as a sacrifice in order to try and appease Molech, a demonic image.

And the list goes on and on. It is our story: how we blame, justify, attack, steal, think we know best and, overall, ignore or destroy anything that exposes us or makes us feel vulnerable. It is the same story told over and over in many different ways.

Chapter 9

"How does it feel to have this longing to be known intimately and yet be a guardian, constantly at work to defend yourself and keep everyone away?" I asked humanity.

Humanity looked away, seemingly lost in thought for a few moments, and then she turned to me, "We don't talk about it."

I pushed a bit harder even though it felt like I was committing an indecency, "If you did talk about it, how has it affected you? What does it mean to carry this struggle in everyday life?"

She had a tired expression and looked around to see who was listening to the conversation. As she saw no one paying attention, she turned back and looked at me. Finally, she said, "You do know you are trying to rip open the devastating secret in each of us? It hurts so much that we take revenge on it by calling names like Nostalgia, Romanticism or even Adolescence."

I had no words to say so she continued.

"Have you ever been in a room of people, where there are little groups of people talking all around you? All of a sudden, a famously beautiful woman walks into the room, and everyone turns to look at her. She commands everyone's attention. There is a collective holding of breath as she slowly moves into the room. As you are staring at her, she looks at you and smiles. Her eyes light up, and she is radiant. She begins to move towards you. Now in that moment," Humanity hesitated for a second and then continued. "In that moment, you know you don't know her. Yet, she noticed you. You want to turn around to see if she is looking at somebody behind you. But the thought that her attention is not on you is too much to bear. In the brief moment, to be special, noticed and yet knowing it is not meant for you, that is what it is like for us."

"So it is like being offered something you want very badly but knowing it is not yours and you can never own it?" I asked.

"Yes, it is a bit like that. It is like going to a doctor who tells you that you have stage 4 cancer and less than a month to live. As you sink into the chair to get your breath, he tells you about a trial drug that could dramatically improve your chances. He only has to determine what your blood type is before moving forward. The mix of despair and hope if you can only pass one hurdle is what it feels like to be us."

"So a despairing death and yet possible hope all at once. All held in IF?" I asked again holding, the "if" as long as I could.

"As soon as you say it or talk about it, it is gone. It is like focusing your attention on being happy. As soon as you focus on it and try and keep it, it is gone," Humanity said with a hint of despair, "It is better not to try and find it at all. It is best to ignore it completely."

"You think that if you got the girl, if the medicine worked, if you were able to get what you saw or felt in the person, medicine, then you would be happy and that is all you would need? What if those things are only the messengers to a far deeper beauty of life being offered to you? What if what you really desired was coming through that person or situation? That longing could not be met by them or the situation but was only a messenger to a deeper life? What if it was God trying to call you back to what you were made for in him?" I asked.

Humanity had a blank look on her face. As if I was speaking in a different language. Then her appearance began to change as she thought I was mocking her vulnerability.

Before I lost all nerve to say anything else I asked, "If you could have anything, what would it be?"

Thankfully, this question settled her down. She smiled a seductive smile and looked at me smugly and echoed my words, "Anything I want? That is easy." She leaned forward and said almost with a hint of bitterness, "I would like to have that desire. To possess it. For it to be mine."

She took a breath and then said strongly, "No, to be the source of that desire. That is what I would want more than anything else in the world. I would gladly give anything to have that power."

The vulnerability of the moment seemed to silence everything. There was an awkwardness in the air. Not knowing what else to do, I thanked her for the time and stood to leave quickly.

Chapter 10

So how does God respond to Adam?
Does he offer any help?

Not the kind we want, that is for sure.

We want this all-powerful God to come storming in
and destroy the one who did this terrible thing to us.

We want a God who will ignore the consequences of
our choices and make everything right.

We want God to pretend how he created us and
what he told us was a lie.

We want decisive action on his part, and we want to
watch him do it all.

After all, he is God and we are just the victims in
this mess.

What does God do?

First, he comes to Adam and asks questions.

That is his help? A God who asks questions?

Before you throw the book down and stomp off mumbling about a "real God who should step up and do something any real 'man' would do," jet's not use ourselves as the standard. Let's see if he has any wisdom to offer us.

Why does he ask a question?

He is the all-powerful God. He is not manipulating us, mocking us or making fun of us. So there is an all-knowing reason why he asks questions.

He is modeling to us the single most powerful tool we have to gain wisdom and understanding.

We have the authority and capacity to investigate, question, explore and discover what only we can learn. Simply put, he is modeling to us, when we are in trouble, ask questions.

The way to gain wisdom and understanding of who we are and what we need to do is to take the gift of guarding, which includes the capacity to question, and use it first and foremost to figure out what the truth is. There is a reason, a rationality in the mind of God to all he does. We are to discover it. There is also a reason and rationality for the things we do, we are also to investigate, explore and discover that.

Remember, he delegated to us this capacity to be like him. A part of that is we must question, explore and investigate in order to learn and grow.

If we didn't have this investigative desire and capacity, we would easily be content with what we know.

That creates a crisis when an infinite God offers us an eternal relationship with him. We will spend all eternity asking questions, exploring, discovering the profound realities of God. There is no limit to it. We are made to learn and grow.

He is saying, "I have placed this capacity in you and I am not going to take it back. Own your life and your choices and figure out what happened. I will walk with you and help you."

The second aspect of what he does continues from this last paragraph: He asks a specific question to help us own our life, "Where are you?" He shows us what key question to start with to find the truth.

When you are dealing with a difficult situation.

When you are working in a changing world.

When you don't know what else to do.

Begin with the question, "Where are you?"

This is the wisdom God offers Adam and Eve right from the start. He is not a bumbling God who asks stupid questions he already knows the answer to. He is modeling to us by what he does. He shows us the first and most basic question to get us back to a real relationship worth guarding with God. It starts by answering the question, where are you?

First and foremost, it is a question of the heart.

A question that is not about which tree he is hiding behind, but about what is going on inside of Adam. God begins with a focus on the heart. He wants Adam to start on the inside and work his way out.

God knows where the real problem is.

He knows we must play our part in dealing with it.

Chapter 11

Where am I?

I am alone. I am on a journey, but I don't know where I am going. I don't even know how to take this journey as it is like no other journey. What do I do?

You are not alone. We are not alone. Whether we admit it or not, we are all on this journey together. The good news is that others have gone before us, and we can learn from them.

Abraham, he is the father of our faith and is a good one to learn from. Where did his journey start?

Leave your country, your people, your father's house…

Our journey begins where Abraham's journey began: "Leave."

I know, I can already hear the words forming: "BUT…"

There is no "but" in this journey. It is a starting place for all of us. We must leave our family and culture behind. Our country, our people and our family are so comfortable, so safe, so known. There are so many places for the heart to hide.

You can't move beyond the "but" yet? Okay, let's look at them.

"But, my family knows me. Surely they could teach me more about myself than anyone else!"

Yes, they know you, and here we must be very careful with our words. They know you in that they have wiped you, fed you, burped you and seen more of you than anyone else in the world. But do they know your heart?

All families are broken. All children growing up in families learn the ways of broken families. There is broken communication, power struggles, jealousy, conditional love, and insecurity, to name a few expressions of the heart.

What did they teach you about dealing with conflict?

How did you earn their love?

Where did you hide to protect yourself?

How much of your heart died to keep peace in the family?

What did they expect of you that was not really "you"?

But what about respecting your family as a part of the Ten Commandments?

You are to honor them as a source of your life and those who have given sacrificially to bring you up. Yes, please respect them, but to respect someone is different from a willingness to let them hold you captive to their desires or expectations. Families are God's idea and very important, but they were never meant to be the place we hide or the source of defining who we are.

Jesus recognized this challenge for us and goes as far as to say we are to "hate" our father and mother in the sense of not letting them hold us captive or define us and our relationship with God.

Adam, before sin entered the world, was told that a man should leave his father and mother and join his wife. He was not to hold his parents above his wife, and he had to leave them in order to join his wife in his heart.

We can see this need to leave at a national level as well. The people of Israel spent 400 years in Egypt. Leeks and onions were a refined taste they developed and learned to love. They learned the strength of horses and chariots. Even though the Israelites eventually became the Egyptians' slaves, it was a safe place for them. One whole generation was lost because, although they physically left Egypt, they still carried Egypt in their hearts. Whenever they got into trouble, they wanted to run back to Egypt.

If you really want to answer your "but," then you have to go behind the question and dig a bit deeper.

What you are concerned about?

What are the feelings you have about this? For you see, it really is a question of the heart.

How do you know when to leave your country, your people and your father's house?

It is not my role to answer that question for you. It is a question of the heart and only God can answer it. They may go with you on a journey to the heart, but you cannot take them with you. That is a choice they must make, and you must guard your own heart and take your own journey.

All journeys have a leaving.

If you don't leave someplace, you never can move on.

Have you left your family, community and culture on your journey to the heart?

Chapter 12

God puts within Abraham's heart the desire to find a city whose maker and builder is God. He gives him an inheritance to be the father of the nations. That, through him, the nations will be blessed.

Now this is no small desire. It will shape his life and be the focus of much of what he does. As we look at it, we think it is only about the inheritance.

But if you read the story carefully, it is not about what God is going to do through him that is the true focus of the story.

It is God using what he is going to do through him to get Abraham's attention and deal with his own issues of the heart.

We must remember that God's focus is the heart. That is truly the focus of the guardian's work and a restoration of our true inheritance.

God gives you desires that are beyond your capacity to reach.

Now if that doesn't frustrate you, I don't know what will. See, if you try to do it on your own, you will fail. If you don't try it, you will be frustrated at not attempting to do what you really want to do.

So how did God use Abraham's inheritance to get to his heart?

Abraham was on his way to Negev and lived there for a while. One day the king, Abimelech,[2] saw Abraham's wife Sarah and wanted to take her as his own.

Abraham was confronted with a painful choice. If he said she was his wife and Abimelech couldn't have her, he feared he would be killed. However, Sarah was vital to his inheritance, as it was through her that God said he would bring a child to fulfill his promise of using them to bless the nations.

Abraham gave in and guarded his own life above his wife's or any inheritance. He gave Sarah to Abimelech.

Abimelech took his new prize and returned home.

God rudely intervened that night in Abimelech's plans and gave him nightmares about what he would do if he touched her and didn't return her to Abraham right away. The king woke up and went quickly to Abraham, asking, "What have you done to us? And how have I sinned against you, that you have brought on me and on my kingdom a great sin?

Finally, in exasperation, he asked Abraham, "What were you thinking when you did this?"

Abraham replied, "You don't know who God is. There is no respect for him and what he is doing here, and besides you would have killed me if I said no."

Generations after Adam stood up to God and blamed him for being the source of the problem, Abraham continued abusing our very special gift. He blamed the people for the condition of his heart and thus guarded himself from shame or guilt.

The odd thing is that there really was the fear of the Lord in the king, because as soon as he found out what God wanted, he did it immediately. The problem truly was that there was not enough fear of God in Abraham. His heart was the problem.

But he couldn't see that as he was too busy protecting himself from the painful revelation of his own cowardly heart.

Chapter 13

Saul was a foot taller than anyone else in Israel. The added space he took up was not wasted. He was Brad Pitt on steroids. To look at him was to stare at him. He was a man's man, and of course that made him desirable by all.

However, he had a heart problem. He was from the smallest tribe and the smallest family of the smallest tribe.

So how can a man who is desired by all, who has everything many of us want, have a heart problem?

I mean, if we just had what we wanted, then everything would be all right... right?

Hmmmm, it doesn't seem like it if history tells us anything.

Adam himself was perfect, and yet he had this problem. How can a man made from dust, yet who has the breath of God and thus the very essence of God in him develop heart problems?

It seems to be a mystery that even God wonders about as he deals with us. On several different occasions, God speaks to his beloved dust man and says to him,

"Why, when I expected it to produce good grapes, did it produce worthless ones?"[3]

"What injustice did your fathers find in Me, that they went far from Me and walked after emptiness and became empty?"[4]

Paul writes about it and calls it, "The Mystery of Lawlessness."[5]

It is not a mystery in the sense of we don't know "Who done it?" It is a mystery in the sense that we can't explain why we do it. There really is no logical reason to choose death over life. If God can't explain it, I will not try myself.

So we are left with the mystery of our own foolishness. Why? Because our heart's motive seems to be the last thing we want to see.

The heart whines to us, "I am trying my best…"

It complains to us, "I couldn't help it…"

It confidently declares to us, "We are all basically good people…"

It whispers seductively to us, "No one understands you…"

The journey to the heart is not for the simple-minded or foolish.

It is not for the blind or arrogant.

It is not for those who are hard of hearing.

It is not for the soft and spoiled or those who are indifferent.

Those who are apathetic, full of themselves, desperately wanting to please others or simply those who don't care, this journey is not for you.

Saul, the first king of Israel, was torn between the journey to the heart and being a traditional king that the people wanted. Which did he choose? How would we view his leadership?

From our view, we see that God used him to build the 12 tribes into a powerful nation.
He was baptized by the Spirit of God.
He had great ancestors who included Abraham, Israel and Moses.
He was a prophet, and the Spirit came on him in power and authority.
He was a leader chosen by God with power from God.
He reigned for 40 years.[6]

However, in the Kingdom of God, Saul was a coward and lost his inheritance.

He chose power to protect himself and turned a blind eye to his heart. His own heart's defense took priority over everything else. Slowly, his shameful heart ate away at him.

He soon would throw spears and try to pin David to the wall.

Then he would gather his army and chase him through the desert to kill him.

Murder was easily justifiable as he was the king and he was only trying to protect what God gave to him.

Jealousy slowly ate away at him. More power was the only medicine that could ease the pain of his pathetic heart.

Seeking out a witch for direction seemed a way forward when he could no longer hear from God.

You can never judge a man by his appearance. There is a vast difference between a man who is "used" by God, who does the "work" of God in the power of God as we see it, and a man who has the courage to do the inner work of the Spirit and gain a transformed heart in the process of doing the work of God.

We may never be able to tell the difference between these two men, but God knows.

One group is heroes in the Kingdom of God, men of whom the world is not worthy. Some will be persecuted, torn in two and die in caves and jails, unknown by the world. Still other heroes will be entertainers, great politicians, teachers, health care workers, fathers, mothers, bankers and artists.

The other group is full of cowards whose only reward in the Kingdom of God will be the minimum wage they are paid here through the shallow praise of those around them. They carry a slowly hardening, diseased heart and guard it as if it were their only treasure. They are a pile of dying bones, dead men walking, who are dark shadows, mists passing through, a waste of a wonderful gift given. Oh yeah, and they may also be entertainers, great politicians, teachers, health care workers, fathers, mothers, bankers and artists.

The one thing you must have more than anything else is a brutal love of the truth, even if it means admitting your heart is corrupt. This includes a longing for authenticity and courage to not give up.

Chapter 14

Imagine a drink so beautiful and seductive that if you even tasted it you would never want anything else. It would become your sole focus and desire.

So what was the sweet nectar our hearts tasted? What is the taste we got a hold of that spoiled us for anything else? What is our craving, our longing, our "heart's desire"?

The serpent's words were simple, "You will be like God, knowing…"

The nectar that poisoned our hearts was the idea that we could be as God. We would know things that only God could know. We wouldn't just be the recipients of life; we could be the center of life.

The serpent twisted what God had given to us and changed our focus. God had already made Adam and Eve in his image. It was a done deal. We were made in his image in regards to our character and capacity to choose life and guard that life.

The twist came when the serpent focused this natural desire to be like God into a desire to be God --like him in his nature. Power, knowledge, authority were to be ours, and we would need nothing from anyone.

The heart tasted this nectar of being God and was immediately spoiled for being a dust man. To be needy, weak, vulnerable, dependent, exposed was now unspeakably foolish.

Add to that the admission that we were rebels against God with the guilt and shame of our rebellion, and the heart wanted no part of being a dust man.

My heart, your heart, your family's hearts, the hearts of all the people in your culture have one single, simple desire: It has tasted the nectar of power and will not settle for anything less.

Our fallen, broken heart will ask us to use this wonderful gift to protect and defend it from the sad, pathetic life of weakness and vulnerability found in being a dust man. It wants us to focus on getting any power we can as a means to move ahead in life and to protect ourselves.

If we do this, there will be consequences.

Chapter 15

There is a small problem with seeking power and trying to be God as a dust man.

We are not God and never will be. It leads to a life of constant struggle, as what we long to be can never be attained.

However, the nectar of this illusion has a strong power over us. It requires the strongest potion to break it.

What does God do to get our heart's attention and break apart the illusion?

Actually, he doesn't have to do anything.

He simply waits.

We will do it all ourselves. We create a world where our heart is the focus of our choices. Our heart's desire is expressed in:

Greed / Power / Jealousy / Envy / Strife / Lust / Coveting

And then, no surprise here, we produce broken relationships, broken families, broken communities and broken nations.

I'm assuming I don't need to go into any details, as all you need to do is look around you.

What is happening in your relationships?

Your family?

Your community?

Your economy?

The politics of your nation?

You can get angry with God all you want, but we have already covered that aspect of the heart.

Truth be known, all we are left with is the fruit of our own choices.

Believe it or not, this is the good news. This is where God steps in and tries to help. God uses the fruit of our choices as a jolt to awaken us. God uses the pain and suffering of our world to get the attention of humanity's deaf and dying heart. God whispers to us through our pleasure, but shouts to us through our pains.[7] Until the arrogant heart finds evil unmistakably present, often in the form of pain, it is enclosed in the illusion of its own invulnerability. It is blind to the reality of its behavior with regards to the laws of the universe and its maker.

When there is pain and suffering, it only confirms and reveals the condition of our heart. Sadly, it is the last place we look to discover what is wrong with us.

Chapter 16

You have an enemy that is focused on and committed to your destruction.

And no, I am not talking about your heart this time. I am talking about another enemy as cunning as your heart. The world is not a neutral place. There is a current, a wind, a movement against developing a whole and healthy heart. It is demonic, and Satan is the one pushing it forward. Let me give you an example. Think of a painful time in your or loved ones' life. It will be even clearer if it deals with injustice. What was the question that came to your mind in the midst of this difficult time? I have taught all over the world, and in every culture and group, with almost anyone I have been with, the question sounds something like this:

Why God?
How could you let this happen?

Why does this question come to all of us in painful times?

The devil is the original dirty fighter. He waits for us to be in a painful situation and then kicks us when we are down. How? He lies to us. He has one goal. Only one desire. One strategy that defines the focus of all he does. He wants to turn your heart against God. That is spiritual warfare. He knows if he can cause you to withhold your heart from God, it is the beginning of the end of a loving relationship. If he can plant the lie that God is not good, that he can't be trusted, your natural reaction will be to withhold love and trust from him. If you can't trust God, you will naturally have an excuse to defend yourself from him. This will slowly produce a hard heart, cynicism, and indifference to God and his kingdom.

Satan was one of the most powerful and beautiful angels in heaven before he rebelled. He chose arrogance and wanted to take God's place. God kicked him out of heaven and he has been obsessed with getting even with God ever since. His only way to get back at God is to destroy anything God cares about, and we are very high on that list. If Satan can convince us to guard our hearts from God, he knows it will cause God pain, and that brings him a great deal of sadistic pleasure.

Your arrogant heart has an ally, a friend, an advocate for its cause. If your heart is looking for an excuse, there is an enemy of light, the father of lies, who will gladly supply you one.

Choose your heart's friends and counselors wisely. For as your friend's hearts go, so goes your heart.

Chapter 17

Let's go back to Abraham and see how he is doing on his journey to the heart.

God puts a desire in the heart of Abraham to have a child. It seems simple enough, at least to those who have children. But as we have said, God uses all aspects of our life to expose our hearts to us.

Abraham and Sarah assumed that a child promised would be a child delivered, now.

Or at least this month a pregnancy.

Okay, this year, as it takes nine months to give birth.

Another year passes by: 12 months, 52 weeks, 365 days.

Then, ever so slowly, another year.

And then another and another.

The heart doesn't like to be frustrated.

It really doesn't appreciate being disappointed.

When it feels ignored or put off, it becomes angry. After all, it is a matter of the heart, and we all know that matters of the heart are not to be trifled with. At least, not matters of our own heart that is. They are to be guarded at all cost. Taken care of, nurtured and watched over.

Sarah finally decides to take action into her own hands. God seems to have slept in. He seems to have forgotten that her biological clock is moving forward and there are some things that just should not be put off.

She takes her Egyptian slave by the arm and marches into the tent. She calls out, "Abraham."

Abraham turns to look at Sarah, knowing by the tone of her voice what she is going to talk about. He is a bit surprised to see her holding a slave girl out to him, "What is it Sarah?" He asks.

Sarah says, "The Lord is a bit slow on keeping his word to us and seems to have a problem with me. Go, sleep with this slave of mine and perhaps I can have a family through her."

Abraham knows what has brought Sarah to this point. He has heard the words over and over and knows how she feels about having a son. Worn out by it all, he responds, "All right Sarah. I will see if I can give you a child through this slave." Abraham sleeps with the slave girl, Hagar, and she gets pregnant.

When Sarah sees that Hagar despises her, she goes to Abraham and declares, "You are responsible for the injustice and pain I am suffering. Now that Hagar is pregnant, she can't stand me. May the Lord deal with you because of this."

Sarah joins the long lineage of people who blame others for their problems. She uses the gift of guarding to keep her heart safe from any embarrassing self-revelation. She blames Abraham as the source of her problem.

Abraham hears the pain in her voice and knows from his own pain that he can do nothing to ease it.

Although I am sure there were different variables in the challenge they faced with Hagar, we can be sure that the issue of the heart was a key part of it. They both agree it's better to just send Hagar away to die than to deal with the issues of the heart it exposes in them.

Chapter 18

What about men of the Bible who did things right? Let's pick one of whom God speaks very highly.

Job is a great example. God says, "There is no one like him on the earth. A blameless and upright man who fears God and is not involved in evil."

Wow, as far as references go, that's as good as it gets. So how is Job's heart in the challenges he faces?

First attack: In the time it takes to read this page, Job loses everything. A neighboring tribe attacks, a wind destroys his children's house, fire from heaven falls and burns up the sheep. In a matter of minutes, it is all gone.

What was Job's response?

"Naked I came from my mother's womb, And naked I shall return there. The Lord gave and the Lord has taken away. Blessed be the name of the Lord."[8]

Through all this, Job does not sin or blame God. He is no coward. He is no wimp. He has done his heart work and is aware of the battle that is going on.

Second attack: He is hit with serious illness. We find him sitting on a heap of ashes, scraping the pus that oozes out of the sores that cover his whole body. There is no place he can sit or lay down that is not pressing on these boils. He is in agony.

His wife can't bear the pain anymore and finally says to him, "Do you still hold fast your integrity? Curse God and die."[9]

Job responds, "You speak as one of the foolish women speaks. Shall we indeed accept good from God and not accept adversity?"

Dig down deeper in Job's heart, break it apart and crush it with suffering, and he still is no coward. He keeps his heart in check and guards his relationship with God as a priority.

So far, so good. Job has passed his tests and is a model of faith that God holds up to the whole universe. In a world where people run at the slightest hint of being vulnerable, Job doesn't run and hide. He stands firm.

His sickness continues. His friends come and sit silently with him for seven days. Then they start to talk and essentially say, "You are not a righteous man. It is your fault." The ongoing pain wears away at him and finally gets to Job. The depth of his heart is revealed in his dialogue with them. The essence of Job's argument is that he knows better than God and he doesn't deserve this.

Finally, God comes in a whirlwind and asks Job a number of questions. One of the questions was, "Will you condemn me that you may be justified?

Righteous Job gets a revelation of his heart. He sees himself as he never has before. His heart has been exposed in a way that only suffering can do, and he has no place to hide as God asks him this question. His heart has turned on God.

Okay, wait a second, you might say. Give me a break, or maybe I should say, "Can't God give poor Job a break? All this suffering just to prove a point about the heart." Job responds great twice. I mean, two out of three isn't bad. Job has gone way beyond what any normal man could deal with.

That may be true from our perspective, but how does Job respond once he has seen his own heart? Is he bitter at God for digging so deeply into his heart? How does the story end?

God shows up and asks Job a few questions to help him get perspective on who God is and who Job is as a dust man.

After Job is reminded of who God is, he says, "You are incredible, God. I had only heard rumors of who you are compared to what I have seen. My heart has deceived me, and I repent of my foolishness."

Job is not offended. He is deeper in love with God and repents of his own heart's foolishness.

Now that is a righteous and God-fearing man who knows what must be guarded at all costs.

Chapter 19

A heart is a funny thing. Not "Ha Ha," but funny/
different and a bit peculiar.

Maybe I have painted a picture that gives the
impression that it is always hiding and can't be
found. But that is not always true. There are times
that it fits into the "dumb sheep" category.

A couple of examples come quickly to mind.

The Israelites are on their way to the promised land.
God has done amazing miracles to get them there
from Egypt. He splits the Dead Sea, and they walk
through on dry land. He provides water in a desert
out of a rock. Finally, they send in 12 spies, who are
leaders among them, to search out the land that God
has promised them. After 40 days, they come back
with amazing stories of the fruit of the land. Then,
they clear their throats a bit and 10 of them say that
there is only one little problem…

"THERE ARE GIANTS IN THE LAND. We are like
grasshoppers in their sight."

Two of the spies, Joshua and Caleb, speak from God's heart and try to convince the people to go in as God is with them.

The people have a choice as to who they will listen to. Who do they choose?

They listen to the 10 spies. This seems to be what their cowardly, narrow-minded, victimized and terrified hearts "knew" to be true. They were terrified, and their dysfunctional hearts were just looking for an excuse not to have to take the risk. They found it in the story the 10 spies told.

The Israelites quickly turn from believing God is bigger than the enemy, and run away from the challenge before them. They refuse to go into the land and, thus, lose their inheritance.

One whole generation is lost and never enters the promised land because they listened to the 10 leaders who were small-hearted men. They wouldn't listen to God speaking through Joshua and Caleb. In the end, they wouldn't deal with what this challenge exposed in them, but avoided the promised land to protect themselves.

Another example is Absalom, David's son.

Absalom would stand outside the court where people who had legal trouble would go to present their cases. As in any court case, the party who the judge decides against is going to feel like there was injustice. In the pain of the loss, it would be much easier to blame others, the system or God instead of deal with what it exposed in them.

Absalom would stand outside and when they came out of court, he would see who was hurting or angry and then he would greet them and say, "I know how painful this is and that no one is listening to you and the grave injustice that has just taken place. I would love to be in a position to give you justice."

Day after day, he would speak to those whose hearts were hurting and who didn't feel like there was justice in the court.

After time, he stole the hearts of the people away from his father the king.

A charismatic leader like Absalom who has a strong family lineage and takes the time to listen is so seductive to the pained heart.

If we are honest, we usually know it is illusions and lies, but we don't want to face ourselves and the reality that this is an imperfect world. We don't want to admit that the people can't do what they say they can; we want to believe them because our hearts are hurting and we don't want to have to deal with it. It is so much easier to blame the leaders, judges and courts than to believe God is at work.

Absalom steals the hearts of the people and then uses the influence to chase his father (the king) out of the kingdom and take over. All he ever wanted was power and control to get his own way.

Beware of leaders (or anyone for that matter) who promise everything you want to hear. In a fallen and imperfect world, no dust man can deliver that.

We don't want to deal with our hearts and turn to God. We want a leader who will take our side and do something for us. Justice, just for us.

Chapter 20

Time drags by for Abraham and Sarah, and God doesn't allow them to get rid of Hagar. God directs her to go back and stay with Abraham and Sarah. Hagar will live with them and be a constant reminder of their own insufficiency. Their inability, weakness and incapacity is clear for all to see.

It is another fifteen years, and Abraham and Sarah are still without their own child.

We don't like anything that makes us vulnerable. Our guardian gift moves immediately to protect ourselves.

What do you do if you have something that is a source of discontent for years?

And years?

And years?

The constancy of a hope or dream denied has a tendency to wear on us. A long, slow, grinding process. It grates on us. It drudges up things in us. It breaks up things that are stuck and exposes painful things beneath it.

We read in Romans, "In hope against hope, he believed in God."[10] Because we idolatrize power, we want to see a strong, determined man who faces the pressure of life, the grinding, grating pressures of faith and stands above it all.

Actually, it is not about the outward appearance of the man at all. When Abraham is 99-years-old, God comes to him again and says he will have a son in the next year. What does this apparently impotent, yet man of faith who is holding onto hope in the face of no hope do?

Abraham fell to his face and laughed.

He then mumbled, "Will a child be born to a man a hundred years old?"[11] He took a breath and said to God, "If only Ishmael might live with this blessing!"

The pain seems to overwhelm him. It is the laugh of someone who is talking about something so painful you either laugh or weep. It is easier to laugh.

His heart seems to expose itself at the deepest level. He is at the end of himself. There is nothing left in him, as he has tried everything. He does what Sarah had done. He asks for the work of his own hands, Ishmael, to be enough.

How long does it take for the heart to declare its need for help? For the gift of guarding to be willing to stop protecting itself and to let a heart be just what a heart is? Painful, needy, broken, weak and in desperate need of being loved. I don't know. It is a question of the heart and the gift of being a guardian. Each one of us must answer that question on our own.

God sees their faith, and a son is born to Sarah and Abraham within the year. Miracles do happen. End of the story, right? No.

Chapter 21

Now, why can't God just leave them alone?
Why does he seem to enjoy rubbing salt in their
wounds?

He gives a man a dream of having a child. The man
is then childless for over 25 years. The dream wears
on him. It slowly crushes him and breaks his heart.
It challenges those he loves and brings them to the
end of themselves. Finally, when they have lost all
apparent hope, a miracle happens and they have a
child. Isaac is born to Sarah.

At last, after all these long and agonizing years, God
gives them what he promised. You would think that
this was enough, that God would finally leave this
poor couple alone and let them raise the child.

What does he expect of us?

What does God want?

What does he do next to Abraham?

If you didn't like the first part, you're going to really hate this. God comes to Abraham and says to him, "Take now your son, your only son, whom you love, Isaac, and go to the land of Moriah, and offer him there as a burnt offering on one of the mountains of which I will tell you."[12]

God has the audacity to now take back what he has promised. He dangles a thread of hope to a childless couple for 25 years and then just as they get used to having this precious little gift around them, just as their starved hearts get used to sharing the joy of this child, God steps in and says, "I want him back, now, and you have to give him as a sacrifice."

This is a test. Maybe the test of all tests. This will expose the heart in ways most of us never even dream of. God has set out a "desire" for the heart to lure it out into the open. Like placing a tasty bit of food in a trap to lure the animal in and capture it. God gives Abraham a desire to have a child and then uses that desire to lure his heart out into the open. To expose it for what it is.

God has taken every option from Abraham's heart. It has no place to hide. Abraham took the bait and loves the child as much as life itself. He has become vulnerable and exposed. He loves something more than he loves his own heart.

Our heart wants to say to Abraham, "Stand up, stop this cruel God from making fun of you. Stop the absurdities of life and protect yourself. No one should have to go through this. You are an old man, grab what is rightfully yours and make a run for it. Don't do it."

But this is our heart's problem. Not Abraham's. What does Abraham do?

He gets up early the next morning and goes on a journey to the mountain called Moriah. He takes the fire, wood and his son. He ties up his son and places him on the alter he built and raises the knife to sacrifice his only beloved son as a gift to his God.

He has finally looked into his heart and faced his fears.

He confronts his fear of death.
Of pain.
Of loss.
Of being cut off and alone.
Of rejection.

Abraham faced his own heart. The source of the problem all along. He abandoned himself to God and didn't guard anything from him.

The guardian has grown up. Twenty-five years of struggle and he is finally willing to trust God with everything that is precious to him. He is finally willing to guard his heart for God. For God alone is worthy. The guardian has returned to his rightful place.

Chapter 22

Remember, Abraham is the gold standard, the working model, the father of our faith. The man that God says to us, "This is how I am going to help you regain what you have lost."

What does God say about that moment and Abraham's willingness to offer up his son?

"...now I know that you fear God, since you have not withheld your son, your only son, from me."[13]

Our willingness to be completely vulnerable, to withhold nothing from God, to trust him with anything and everything that is precious to us, seems to be of such importance to restoring us and building relationships fit for the Kingdom of God that any sacrifice seems a small price to pay for attaining it.

It is as if God says to Abraham, "Your heart must be a visible expression of who you are. It must be expressed in the words you use and your actions. It must be something others can see. I want to see what you do and how you talk as a vulnerable expression of your life in me."

God meant what he said when he called us to become perfect as he is perfect--perfected in love. We are being made into something new, radically new. Not better men, but sons of God. That requires major transformation, and it starts in the heart.

It begins with death. A real abandoning of self. Submit to death--death of your ambitions and wishes every day and, in the end, death of your whole body. Then and only then will you find life, his life, eternal life.

If we learn vulnerability with him in every fiber of our being. If we hold nothing back from him. If we totally abandon ourselves to him. Then, it will be the seeds of life that will grow into the very things we long for.

Nothing in you that has not died will ever be raised from the dead. Look in your heart, and you will find hatred, loneliness, despair, rage, ruin, and decay. But look to God and you will find him, and with him, love, intimacy, joy, life and beauty with so much more.

Chapter 23

Let's return to our heart's struggle.

I want to give you a practical exercise. Read the paragraph below, and keep the focus in mind as you do.

Focus: There have been burglaries in the neighborhood recently, and a family has brought you in to advise them on how to keep from being robbed. The house is in a very wealthy neighborhood. The grass is uncut and has brown spots. The garage is full of tools, toys and is used for household storage. The garage door isn't closed all the way, and its back window is open.

You walk into the house and go through the rooms. There are four bedrooms and three bathrooms, a large kitchen and a beautiful fireplace in the living room. The carpet is clean, and the house is neat except for a small stain on the couch. The curtains are light brown and the living room walls are baby blue. There are pictures of the family hung throughout the hallway. The study is large with a nice desk in the middle and a small safe in the corner. There's a laptop on the desk and bookshelves along the far wall. There are beautiful picture windows that look out at the mountains in the east. One bathroom window is open to let in air.

As you read this, I am going to assume that your primary focus was on areas that could protect the house. Nothing else really mattered.

Now imagine if you were told the people wanted you to come in as an appraiser to help them figure out what they needed to do to sell the house. You would look differently at the entire thing. What you are focused on defines how you view it.

Now hold this thought for a moment. Up until now I have not used any "bad" language. But I have come this far, and it is now time to use strong language. I know you might be offended, but I have to take the risk, as there is no other way to describe the focus of the heart. It is really rather simple, the heart wants (if you are easily offended, please skip this part) CONTROL.

There, I said it. The C word. Most of us will declare we don't have a problem with this. I am not talking about motive here; you can have the best motive in the world and still focus on control.

If the truth be known, I have been talking about control this whole time. It is the primary focus, desire and skill set of the guardian. He is a master of giving the illusion of control.

I can almost hear some of you saying, "Okay, I do have a small control problem every once in a while, but not too often…"

Yes, I know, you have been listening to your heart again, haven't you? For I am not talking about a behavior that happens every once in a while or a thought that we struggle with in certain situations. Oh, if only it were that simple.

Now let me tie the exercise and this section together. I am talking about a whole mindset. The whole frame out of which the guardian wants us to view the world. Every aspect of our thinking and values is unconsciously grounded in this soil. It is the essence of how we see the world around us.

The guardian now has one primary focus and, compared to it, nothing else matters. It is simply looking for power to get control. That defines how it looks at everything and everyone.

Just as you focused on protecting the house in the illustration above and that became your primary focus, so the guardian takes on a focus of protecting the heart with a goal of being safe. In light of this, nothing else matters.

Chapter 24

So what is this mindset, this paradigm or "glasses" out of which our heart uses to see the world?

If you would allow me, I will dip into the pool of research[14] for a couple of chapters to see what is a common use of our guardian gift. There are four common values that are linked to a defensive heart, regardless of race, culture, personality, economic status or how mature you are. Anytime you feel vulnerable or embarrassed, these values automatically kick in as a part of our wonderful gift and oh-so-broken worldview. They are:

Don't expose your heart.

When you feel vulnerable, don't tell anyone what your agenda is. Keep your agenda hidden so others won't know what you are trying to do. I think of David after he committed adultery. Bathsheba gets pregnant, and David brings Uriah, her husband, home from fighting a war in an attempt to get him drunk so that he will sleep with his wife and keep David from being exposed. When that doesn't work,

David sends him back to the front lines where he sets up Uriah's death. Problem solved and no one is the wiser, except God.

You may get the idea that this has only to do with sin and covering it up, but it doesn't. Anytime, in any situation where we feel vulnerable or threatened, even with the best motives, the guardian is at work to protect us by keeping our agenda hidden from others. If others don't know what you are doing or where you are going, they can't expose you.

Define the situation as a competition; work so you win and others lose.

The threatened guardian hates to be vulnerable, so the primary goal is to achieve power and thus protection. When we are threatened, power becomes the issue and a competition is formed. Only the winner gets power, so winning becomes the primary goal and focus. When you have to communicate, only use the information that supports your view and silence any other information that exposes you.

You can see this mentality in the disciples. When they feel vulnerable, they talk about who among them is the greatest. They are captivated by power, and they define who is great among them by who has the most power.

Suppress any feelings that may make you appear vulnerable.

The defensive guardian feels most exposed by feelings and tries to shut off any sharing of them with others. Tell others what you think they want to hear and say it in a way that makes them feel good, even if it is not true. Avoid saying anything to others that might expose them or cause them pain.

Use rationality to convince people you are right.

As you argue your side, treat the problem as if there is only one right answer, your answer. Use your logic as the only true logic; if necessary, swing to an extreme to prove your point.

The Pharisees were really good at this. One time they came to Jesus and asked why his disciples didn't wash their hands when they ate bread. It was not allowed according to the tradition of the elders. They had all the logic and arguments to support their view. The only problem was that it was built on guarding themselves from exposing their hearts.

The challenge in this is that the guardian is so good at guarding itself, we don't even know this is going on. We are master guardians, so unconsciously brilliant that we actually are blind to our own defensiveness.

Don't believe me?

The next time you are embarrassed or feel vulnerable, see if these values are quietly at work behind the scenes in your heart. Take a step back from the situation and reflect on what the heart calls "wisdom" (the above values, not a motive). You will notice these automatic reactions that come from your broken heart trying to protect itself.

Chapter 25

I will assume you have kept reading from the last chapter and haven't yet had time to reflect personally on what happens when the guardian is at work in a threatening situation.

So how might we see these values at work in a way that helps us understand the challenge of working with our heart?

If I might draw specifically from the well of research[15] one more time for this chapter, we can look at what happens in a team when these values are unconsciously at work. The fruit would be:

Loss of trust:

When the heart is hidden, when people don't say what they mean or mean what they say, it creates a lack of authenticity. With that, integrity is lost. If there is a mismatch between what people say and do, then others do not trust them. Trust is the fruit of vulnerability, of knowing someone's heart. When you don't know people's hearts, you won't trust them.

This is why Jeremiah wrote that the man who trusts in God is blessed and the man who trusts in mankind and makes his own protection his strength is cursed. If the guardian is not doing what it was made to do--guarding our relationship with God--but instead guards our hearts from God and others, the fruit of it will be broken and painfully dysfunctional relationships, which is the curse Jeremiah wrote about.

Fear of conflict:

Conflict implies dealing with differences. When things are different, it often makes us feel vulnerable. When we feel vulnerable, we want to know there is a connection, a similarity that will hold us together. That is found in purpose, passion or values. But all those are expressions of the heart and the place where trust is built. When trust is lost, we tend to avoid tension and fear conflict to keep safe. This then creates a culture of conformity, where everyone is expected to "do" the same thing. Soon any type of creativity is lost, as that is seen as being different and thus avoided.

God cuts right across this fear when he challenges us to count it all joy when we have difficult times. For it is through conflicts and challenges that we will be perfected.

Lack of commitment:

If you don't know what people think about a project or even just life, you don't really know them as people, and thus there is no relationship. If this continues, you can feel disconnected from them. This leads to avoiding conflict and grows into an avoidance of commitment. We will not be committed to those we don't know and thus don't trust. Those involved in this situation will tend to avoid commitment, which will further limit relationships and affect communication and any sense of vulnerability.

Avoidance of accountability:

When people feel disconnected from a group or relationship, they feel less responsible for the outcome. If they are disaffected and removed, they care less about results and are less inclined to go above and beyond what is expected. As a result, they won't have difficult conversations about the important issues involved and will avoid accountability to a project or relationship, as there is minimal ownership in it.

Inattention to results:

As people avoid being held responsible for projects or relationships they're not invested in, there tends to be a denial about the real issues and challenges the relationship/team faces.

This process towards ineffectiveness is connected to our inability to communicate from the heart. What seems like a natural response in keeping our hearts guarded in relationships and protecting them from getting hurt spirals into a lack of engagement with the world and a lack of care for how things turn out. It provides insight into why teams and organizations are so ineffective and bureaucratic and shows that, if we are willing to see it, each one of us plays a part in the problems around us.

At the very least, we should be able to see why our marriages, family and churches are so shallow and broken. We won't connect at the heart level to build trust and a strong enough foundation for healthy relationships to grow.

It should also help us to see if we are struggling with our relationship with God, a key aspect is that we are not working from our heart and connecting to God's heart. There is little trust and thus little relationship.

Chapter 26

An adapted quote from C. S. Lewis

To love at all is to be vulnerable.

Love anything, and your heart will certainly be wrung and possibly be broken. If you want to make sure of keeping it intact, you must give your heart to no one, not even to an animal. Wrap it carefully round with hobbies and little luxuries, avoid all entanglements; lock it up safe in the casket of your selfishness. But in that casket--safe, dark, motionless, airless--it will change. It will not be broken; it will become unbreakable, impenetrable, irredeemable. The alternative to tragedy, or at least to the risk of tragedy, is damnation. The only place outside Heaven where you can be perfectly safe from all the dangers and perturbations of love is Hell...

We shall draw nearer to God, not by trying to avoid the sufferings inherent in all loves, but by accepting them and offering them to him; by throwing away all defensive armor in our relationship with him.   If our hearts need to be broken, and if he chooses this as the way in which they should break, so be it.

Chapter 27

We must track the heart.

I know that sounds ridiculous as our heart is in us. So why bother?

The heart wants to stay hidden and will not expose itself unless it has to. Even if we know the values it lives by and how it affects our relationships, we still have to do the work of connecting to our heart, and that begins with learning to track it.

How do we track it?

We look for its scent. We look for what clues it leaves behind to tell us what is going on. The scent to the heart is most often found through emotions. There is an old saying, "Where there is smoke, there is fire." If you see smoke, you can know with certainty that there is a source. So it is with the heart; if you can be aware of your emotions, you know the heart is around somewhere.

Most of us just classify emotions into two categories: good and bad. All we are really saying is that we like certain emotions and we don't like others.

Many people only want the "good" emotions. So they shut down any feelings associated with pain, hurt or suffering as it makes them feel vulnerable. However, they expect to still enjoy the "good" feelings.

Sorry, but this is not the way the heart works. It has one conduit or "pipe" for emotions. If you close the pipe to limit the pain of certain emotions, then all the emotions are cut off and you stop feeling anything. When this happens, the heart slowly chokes to death. If you want to feel love, joy and passion, you must also be vulnerable to being hurt, disappointed and cut off.

No emotion is good or bad in itself. All emotions are just that: emotions. They are expressions of, or "scents," given out from the values of the heart. The essence of the heart has to do with values. Whatever you treasure, that is where your heart will be.

These heart treasures will find expression in emotions that might include fear, passion, desire, longing and delight. These are all emotions that are dripping with the heart's values. You can't separate values from emotions, as the thing that makes values truly powerful is the emotions that are connected to them.

Think of these words as emotions:

Fear, desire, lust, envy, concern, passion, hate, dread, delight, anxiety, worry, longing, unease, joy, love.

As we experience them in our world, each gives an awareness of what is going on in your heart and thus in your relationships.

Just admitting that you feel bad gives you almost no useful information of what's going on in your heart. On the other hand, knowing precisely what you feel gives you very clear feedback about where you are.

For instance, look at these emotions below. They are similar emotions in a string but have a stronger intensity as you move to the right.

disappointed - sad - grieving

satisfied - happy - thrilled - ecstatic

concerned - upset - anxious - hysterical

curious - interested - aroused - lustful - obsessed

disapproving - angry - furious[16]

To know "where you are" will give you insight into what is going on in your heart. As you are aware of that, it is much easier to know how to engage others and to be aware of what you are looking for or reacting against in the relationship.

A warning must be given here: This is messy, not always black and white, and logic doesn't always reign. The whole issue with emotions is about control and being vulnerable. That is the issue we will all find ourselves confronted with.

Thankfully, we do have a standard in God, so we can see how he deals with his and our emotions. A wonderful scripture in the Psalms says that God collects our tears and puts them in a bottle. Now if God is so interested in our tears, then we have to admit that our tears--read: heart feelings--have great importance because they are connected to our hearts and he is very interested in our hearts.

God is very clear as he shares his heart with us. Listen for the emotions in these scriptures.

"How can I give you up, Oh Ephraim? How can I surrender you, Oh Israel? How can I make you like Admah? How can I treat you like Zeboiim [Sodom and Gomorrah]? My heart is turned over within Me; all My compassions are kindled."[17]

"The Lord your God is in your midst, a victorious warrior. He will exult over you with joy; he will be quiet in his love; he will rejoice over you with shouts of joy."[18]

"Then the kings of the earth and the great men and the commanders and the rich and the strong and every slave and free man hid themselves in the caves and among the rocks of the mountains; and they said to the mountains and to the rocks, 'Fall on us and hide us from the presence of him who sits on the throne, and from the wrath of the Lamb; for the great day of their wrath has come, and who is able to stand?'"[19]

Learning to listen to our emotions, not to just react, is learning to understand and work from the heart. Dealing with emotions also helps us understand God, as it gives us understanding into his heart and how he might feel about things. Remember, we are made in his image. Emotions are an important part of being an image bearer.

Chapter 28

The mind is such a wonderful gift.

We have spent hundreds of years focusing on it and making it the center of our attention. You know the, "I think, therefore I am."

It's such a wonderful machine: You put information in, run it through an analysis and out comes the logical output. It is so safe and certain... and also limited.

The limitation is that the mind has an ally, a source from which it works its magic. The mind draws its resources from another place: the heart.

The mind can only see, focus on and analyze the material the heart allows it to.

If the heart will not accept something, it will refuse to look in a direction,

If it will not recognize the value of something than it doesn't want,

If it wants to feel one way even though facts say something else,

If it has been hurt and is nurturing the pain,

If the heart just doesn't like something,

Then it is the mind's work to logically explain the desires of the heart.

The heart that refuses to deal with pain or focuses solely on its own pleasure will become hard or calloused. This condition bends and twists the mind to shape how it wants the world to be.

The conscience whispers that we should not focus just on our desires and harden our heart, so the heart must find a way to protect itself. Voila, it creates an argument that is wonderfully logical but skewed.

An example will help: "The scribes and the Pharisees were watching Him closely to see if He healed on the Sabbath, so that they might find reason to accuse Him."[20]

Their hearts wanted to find something to judge Jesus with and thus a way to excuse themselves. It was against the law to heal on the Sabbath, which gave them an opportunity to accuse him of breaking the law. Here was a man doing miraculous things and everyone was admiring him. At the same time, he was putting them in a light they didn't want. This made them vulnerable.

How did they respond to this exposure? Their defensive hearts focused their thinking, expectations and what they looked for. We see this over and over in the lives of those who didn't want to hear what Jesus was saying or who he was. It was much easier to destroy him than deal with what he exposed about them.

Futility of the mind can be an expression of a hard heart. That is why the Bible talks of people who have ears to hear but cannot hear and eyes to see but cannot see. Their hearts guard them from seeing what they don't want to see.

If your heart doesn't want to deal with something, you won't deal with it or even talk about it. It is a type of blindness or darkness.

If you are not connected to your heart, if you are not aware of it and dealing with it, then all the logic in the world will not help you, for the problem is not logic but a heart that won't be vulnerable.

Chapter 29

I can almost hear some people grumbling and complaining when we talk about being vulnerable and working from the heart.

"It's not fair."
"What God is asking of us is too much."
"It's not possible to deal with the heart in the world we live in."
"No one can do what God is asking."
"It will never work in the real world."
"It's so unnatural and hard."

From our perspective, that really feels true. We might even feel justified in our "victim" status, as most of our experiences seem to confirm that it is far too dangerous to live this way. Men, in particular, have a difficult time dealing with issues of the heart. To expose our hearts is a recipe for painful humiliation when working with other men.

So how does God think he has the authority to tell us to do this when he has no idea what he is talking about? After all, what does God know about living vulnerable in this crazy world?

I think this is a great argument. God has answered it clearly, in his own way. What is his answer to this core question?

Jesus.

He is the very heart, the DNA, the essence of God's being, the core of all relational reality. He comes to earth to walk, live and model life to us.

God doesn't ask us to do something he is not willing to do or has not done. For that reason, he sent Jesus. What situations was Jesus confronted with that would show us that God understands us and has authority to speak to our lives?

The Almighty, Sovereign God emptied himself and became vulnerable:
He took the form of a fetus.
Was born in a barn.
He was illegitimate.
A refugee.
He didn't have a peer group.
Was raised by a stepfather with step-brothers.
Didn't attend school after 13.
Was a political exile.
Never married, never had sex or kids.
Never owned a home.
Was rejected by his own people.
One of his disciples betrayed him to the authorities for money.
Was arrested unjustly and accused by jealous leaders
He was innocent and his only "crime" was "just being himself."

After giving three years of his life to his disciples, they fled for their lives when there was trouble, and Peter, when questioned, said he didn't even know him.

He died an excruciating death as those who watched it mocked him.

Even though he felt totally forsaken by his father, his dying words were, "(Father) Into your hands do I commit my Spirit."

Jesus models true vulnerability to us. Not some soft, "Oh, kick me again," doormat. Or "I am nothing and have nothing to give." Or "Please don't acknowledge me." But a real, "This is the most valuable, loving, wise way to live and I am not embarrassed about it or backing off from it."

Chapter 30

If Jesus was the heart of God on display among us,
If he was the exact representation of his father so
that if we have "seen" him, we have "seen" his father,
Then how did he try and help those he interacted
with?

Nicodemus –

A Pharisee and a ruler of the Jews. He comes to
Jesus and acknowledges that he is a teacher who
must come from God because of the miracles he is
doing. What does Jesus tell him? Jesus says, "You
must be born again to see the kingdom of God."

Jesus cuts right to the heart of the issue and
challenges Nicodemus at the core of his being.
How? He is a leader who wants to figure it all out.
He thinks he can do it himself, and Jesus tells him
to do something that he can't do in his head. This
will expose his heart and, if there is a desire to really
know God and have his heart revealed, this will take
him to a whole new understanding of his heart and
thus his need for God.

Samaritan woman –

Jesus is tired and rests at a well while the disciples go into town to get some food. As he sits there, he has a conversation with a Samaritan woman. Jews are not supposed to even associate with these people, and Jesus engages her in conversation.

He begins by asking for a drink of water and finally says to her, "You have had five husbands, and the man you are with now is not your husband." Her heart is exposed, and she continues in the conversation to discover who Jesus really is. Jesus sees the desire of her heart to be loved and the pain of not finding this love in men, and he directs her to the true source of love.

A man sick for 38 years –

Jesus is in Jerusalem and goes to Bethesda, a pool where sick people would go to get well. A sick man has been waiting there 38 years but can't seem to get into the water quick enough to get healed.

Jesus asks him, "Do you wish to get well?" What a brilliant question. After all these years, the man will have defined himself by his disability. He will only know how to relate to others as a disabled man. Jesus cuts right to the heart and asks him if he really wants to get well. Is he willing to stop focusing on the disability and deal with the heart that the healing will expose?

If you read the rest of the story, the man is not really ready to get well and deal with his heart. When asked right after the miracle why he is carrying his mat on the Sabbath, he blames Jesus and won't deal with his own heart.

Another time, the Scribes and Pharisees come to Jesus with a woman caught in adultery.

Jesus simply states, "Let him who is without sin throw the first stone." Their hearts are so exposed by such a statement that eventually all of them slip away and hide.

As he talks with his own disciples, he explains everything to them and works hard to help them deal with issues of the heart. He explains to them that power and control are the issues in leadership and therefore they must be servants.

As you read about his life, all his interactions and relationships were rooted in getting to, exposing or capturing the heart of the people he was dealing with and rebuilding a trusting relationship.

Chapter 31

An outfit is a very important part of a job.

I think immediately of a policeman and the uniform he wears. When you see someone in a police uniform, you automatically know the job and purpose. He or she is there to protect the people and to make the community as safe as possible.

The strength of law enforcement, and thus a key part of government, rests on people trusting those in the uniform to perform their duty. When that trust is in the uniform, people get the message and everyone's quality of life improves. The government becomes stronger.

However, when a man or woman wears a uniform but is corrupt and steals, deals drugs, hides the truth or closes an eye regarding certain people and their actions, the trust in uniform is lost. The government is weakened and will eventually be destroyed if the corruption is not dealt with.

So, in light of this, what is the uniform for the Kingdom of God?

How are we to represent the will of God by the uniform/actions of our lives?

If we read the Bible, there seems to be one clear message from God. If you are going to express allegiance to his Kingdom, you must do it his way. His way is working from the inside out. Love requires a uniform of vulnerability.

God tells of his pain in working with people who say they are his and then worship idols, are involved with sorcery and offer their children as a sacrifice to appease the gods around them.

He expects this of the lost, but for those who go by his name, his judgment is swift and harsh. This is the story of the Old Testament. God gave Israel a way to live that would give them all the blessings he had for them.

The problem was that they kept some of the outward appearance but didn't deal with their hearts. Thus they were just actors wearing the clothes of religion while they cheated, stole and defrauded each other behind the scenes.

In the New Testament, Jesus gets the angriest at the religious leaders who go by the name of God and represent his authority, but do not do the work of God.

In the Kingdom of God, you focus on humility and embracing a contrite and broken heart. As you do that, grace, mercy, forgiveness and love find more and more expression in your life.

That is the Kingdom of God.

You don't have to be perfect. In fact, you have a growing awareness that your heart is not, so you don't hide it; you discover in Jesus there is grace and you walk that grace out in your life. And because you have received grace, you give it freely to others.

However, to say you are a part of God's Kingdom and to not try working from the heart is disastrous for us and agony to him. In our walk with God, we are either moving towards vulnerability or away from it.

The Pharisees represented those who had developed this hypocrisy, or moving away from vulnerability, to a fine art. This hypocrisy is the one thing that seems to anger God more than any other thing.

Why do I say that? Look at Jesus' relationship with the Pharisees. He loved them as much as any other people. But they had the audacity to claim a status with God that was based on their actions, rather than on their heart's connection to him.

God's people must represent his heart, or his Kingdom will be seen as twisted, distorted and possibly even corrupt. Then the Kingdom of God will eventually lose influence with many people because they think they can't trust him. Those who claim to walk with him and yet lack vulnerability will only alienate others and confuse people about God.

We are the only image of God many people may see, and if it doesn't include vulnerability, we are misrepresenting God.

Jesus lay down his life to establish, restore and build that trust. So for God, it is a very serious thing to lose the trust that cost him so much. God is committed to building a Kingdom of trust and working from the heart out. If you don't understand this, you will not understand God and his Kingdom at all.

Listen to Jesus' words to the Pharisees:

"Serpents, you brood of vipers! How can you escape the sentence of hell?"[22]

"...They are blind guides of the blind."[23]

"But woe to you, scribes and Pharisees, hypocrites, because you shut off the kingdom of heaven from people; for you do not enter in yourselves, nor do you allow those who are entering to go in."[24]

"...you clean the outside of the cup and of the dish, but inside they are full of robbery and self-indulgence. You blind Pharisee, first clean the inside of the cup and of the dish, so that the outside of it may become clean also."[25]

"He said to them, 'Rightly did Isaiah prophesy of you hypocrites, as it is written: 'This people honors Me with their lips, But their heart is far from Me. And in vain they worship Me. Teaching as doctrines the commandments of men.'""[26]

Jesus says the Pharisees' hearts were focused on doing all their good works in order to be seen by men. They professed loyalty to the Kingdom of God but would not work from the inside out towards a worthy God, and Jesus was vehemently opposed to them.

The Pharisees were students of the law. They studied it and wanted to make it a part of their lives. But the problem was they hid behind the law, instead of using it to reveal their heart and their need for God.

The law was given not to make us righteous, but to lead us to the true state of our heart. The law was given to expose us for what we really are: corrupt, lost, rebellious and shameful with no hope in ourselves.

That is where the Kingdom of God begins.

What does he do with corrupt, lost, rebellious and shameful sons and daughters?

He offers his heart - Jesus' life as a replacement for us and gives us a new heart to live out of: His. If you don't get that, you don't get the Kingdom of God, for the Kingdom of God is within you. Vulnerability is how you find it.

Chapter 32

"Everything is great," Mark stated.

"That sounds good. Just as a curiosity, what would happen if it wasn't?" I asked.

"Can't I just be happy?"

"Sure, but humor me, dig a bit beneath it. What would happen if you weren't happy?"

"I don't like being sad. It seems wrong."

"Wrong, what does that mean?"

"Wrong, like there is something wrong. That is all I mean."

"Wrong with you?"

"Yes, if I am sad, then it means something is probably wrong with me. If something is wrong with me..." Mark hesitated.

"You are doing great, keep going, if something is wrong with you, then how do you feel?"

"Then I feel cut off, distant, and I don't like that," Mark replied.

"Where did you learn that if something is wrong, then you are cut off, distant or, can I add, rejected?"

"Rejected? Hmmm, yes, maybe a bit. Never thought of it that way. I feel like people won't like me if they think something is wrong with me."

"And where did you learn this?" I asked.

"In my family. We were a very competitive family. My dad came alive when we won or distinguished ourselves in a sport. If you didn't win or succeed, you weren't acknowledged."

"So what did you learn from this?"

"I guess I learned that if you don't succeed or win, you are a nobody and no one who matters will acknowledge you."

"So where might you find your value?"

"It looks like I connect my value to succeeding or winning."

"And what might that mean about how God sees you?" I asked.

"I don't know, I haven't thought about this," Mark replied.

"Sounds like a great place to begin a new conversation with God about how he loves you and where you hide or try to defend yourself from him. Can you make the link to being happy? Happy means good, successful, winning, being loved?"

"Okay, that is enough for now. It wears me out just thinking about it, but I will reflect on it more. Thank you."

Chapter 33

So what happened to the gift of the guardian?

There are two basic, unconscious expressions you
could make. One is not better than the other; they
are just different expressions of the same thing. Two
sides of the same defensive coin.

The first response is to hide, which happens about
80% of the time.

You can be so well guarded that you never really
reveal who you are. You hide the real you and never
let anyone else see you. In fact, you don't even know
who you are, as you have guarded yourself so well
that you have forgotten what you hid.

You hide in the expectations of others. You find out
what your parents or culture wants you to be and
you become it. You study hard, you go to church.
You don't swear, wear the right clothes and don't
rock the boat. You are safe because when you are
what others expect you to be, they won't hurt you.

You hide in education or a relationship.

You hide in books or movies of others' imaginations.

You hide in your marriage or your children.

You hide behind a job or the things you own that others approve of.

You hide behind music with earplugs snug in your ears and no other sounds allowed in.

You are slowly killing yourself. A frog in slowly boiling water. No risks, no expressions of the heart, no courage to step out, just the safe, boring, same mundane steps over and over. You have created a safe jail cell that ends up holding you captive.

The second response is that you became a warrior, which happens approximately 20% of the time.

It is a kill or be-killed world. Only the strong survive. Everything is a fight, to the victor goes the spoils

It seems odd to say, but you are still hiding, you just become aggressive. You say what you think, you speak up and vent the pent-up feelings and it seems like they all come out, all at once. Like a cornered cat, you take your claws and vent what seems to be killing you. It may not last long before you get it all out and then go back into hiding.

You rarely reveal anything personal of the heart, as that would make you vulnerable.

The guardian is brilliant at using these two areas. If one doesn't work, switch to the other, or use a deadly combination.

The hard part is that we are brilliant at seeing others being defensive and usually blind when it is in us.

In the New Testament, this being blind would eventually, if not dealt with, work out in us a love for darkness. For men love darkness. What that means is that darkness is the perfect "cover" for the heart. No one can find you unless you want to be found. And even then, it is on your own terms.

The New Testament writers made it very clear that we are to cast off the works of darkness:

To take no part in the unfruitful works of darkness, but instead expose them.

We are to wrestle with the current powers of darkness.

As we are delivered from the domain of darkness.

To hate others is to choose darkness, which will blind us.

If you could summarize the work of the guardian, the misplaced use of this precious gift, it is to keep us in the dark and others in the dark about us.

In the darkness, no one knows what you are doing. No one knows who you are. Any context for how to evaluate you has been removed. It is the perfect place to hide, if you don't want to be exposed for what you are.

Chapter 34

"Excuse me sir, are you a zealot?" I asked.

"Yes I am, I care passionately about the truth God has given to us," he replied.

"I noticed you were with this group. They just stoned that man for not agreeing with you. They lay their garments at your feet for you to watch over while they did this. You seemed to take great pleasure in their trust of you as they cast their stones at the man," I stated with a bit of nervousness.

"Yes, I am one of them. A leader amongst them. Did you notice the arrogance of that man? He truly deserved to be stoned for his arrogance. He declared to have seen heaven open and the Son of Man standing at the right hand of God. He called us disobedient." The face of the man began to grow red with anger as he said these last words.

"I also noticed he cried out, 'Lord, do not hold this sin against them' as he died," I pondered aloud. "Seems like he really cared for you to say such a thing."

The zealot turned to face me with an angry face, "What are you saying? Are you taking his side and saying we are not righteous men?"

"How would you describe righteousness? What makes you righteous?" I asked.

"We have the Law of God. We are a chosen people. We have been obedient to that our whole life."

"What about the heart?" I asked, "What is the condition of your heart?"

The zealot reached down to pick up a stone, and I quickly turned and fled.

I later learned that this young zealot was consumed with destroying anyone connected with the man they stoned. He was committed to destroying anyone who dared to say he needed forgiveness for anything. His own heart was well-guarded in his zeal to destroy others and appear righteous.

• • •

"Excuse me, are you the same zealot I talked with months ago?" I asked.

"Yes, I am," he replied.

"How is the hunting going? Have you found more men to destroy?" I wondered if the rumors I had heard were true.

"Hmmmm, interesting you should ask. Let me say I was wrong about them. You could say I saw the light. They were right, and I was wrong. I am now zealous for them. I am going to build a strong community to help them understand the faith they have," he replied.

"How is your heart?" I asked again.

"I will show them I am one of their apostles, maybe the least of them, but one of them. I will show you this in the years to come," he replied as he walked off, busy to plant churches.

• • •

"Hello Mr. Zealot. How are you? I haven't seen you in years."

"Hello, yes it has been years."

"How is your work going?" I asked.

"It is going well. We have churches planted in the major cities and are growing quickly."

"How is your leadership in these churches?"

"Difficult, to say the least. There are challenges all around, sleepless nights, prosecution. I am lied about and have no place to lay my head," he replied.

"How is your heart?" I asked again.

"Odd you should ask. It is grieved at the hardness of hearts. As to the law, I am guiltless; no one would dare accuse me of any wrongdoing. But I have seen things in my life that trouble me. My response is not always the best response, and I need help. I would go as far as to say I am the least of the saints. But if you will excuse me, there is more work to do," he stated as he walked on to care for the communities of faith.

• • •

"Mr. Zealot, is that you? I would hardly recognize you. How are you?"

The zealot wept for a few moments. "The burden of my God is upon me. I long for the people to know the intimacy I have discovered. It weighs on me. It grips me. I am consumed by his love and grace for all mankind."

"You are not angry anymore. What happened?"

"Yes, the anger is long gone. I have looked deep into my heart and saw past my own righteousness."

"I know you will die soon, how is your heart?" I asked.

"My heart is corrupt. I am the worst of all sinners. I am not better than anyone else."

"How did you discover this? You went from a man who would kill others who disagreed with you to a man who identified with them and saw himself no better than others."

"Yes, I've noticed you have been watching me. Why don't you come and follow Jesus?" He asked with a smile.

"What do I do to know the condition of my heart?" I asked.

"Ask the God who became a dust man to reveal it to you. Ask in faith that he will show you your condition and then watch it as life comes along to reveal it to you. I must warn you, it is not a pretty sight. You should study his heart, for it is only in knowing his heart that you can find the grace to know your own heart. It is good for the heart to be strengthened by grace."

"What is your name?" I finally asked.

"I am sorry, I thought you knew. I am Paul, a servant of God."

Chapter 35

A quote from C. S. Lewis

We are half-heart creatures...

If we are to be honest and take God at his word in
regards to the unblushing promises he has made
for us, if we are to stop and realize the rewards
promised in the Gospels, it seems obvious that our
God finds our desires not too strong, but pitifully
weak.

We are half-hearted creatures, distracted by
drinking, sex and our heart's blind ambition when
infinite joy is offered us.

We are like an ignorant child who wants to go on
making mud pies in a slum because he cannot
imagine what is meant by the offer of a holiday at
the sea.

We are far too easily satisfied.

Chapter 36

You may be tempted to think after reading this far in the book that God gets great joy out of crushing, breaking, annihilating and destroying our hearts, and if that happens, then he is happy.

We do seem to naturally move towards a bent and twisted view of God, and this would fit in clearly with our heart's natural tendency.

You might even be tempted to think that we are not to have any boundaries and just to "let it all hang out."

Firstly, God made it clear to us in giving us his son that he is good and loves us with an everlasting love.

However, it is important to make it clear that his end goal is not to break our hearts. We have already done that without any help from him.

The problem is that we are so threatened by being vulnerable that we avoid admitting it at any cost. What he is really trying to deal with in all of this is our arrogance in hiding and refusing to be honest about where we are.

God wants to restore the proper use of our gift of guarding to its rightful place. Dealing with and exposing our broken hearts is only a means back to the goal of a vulnerable intimacy with him.

It is only when God has taken the place he is worthy of in our hearts that we can truly begin to have healthy and appropriate boundaries. This is the fruit of a guardian doing what it was made for.

When God is the center of our attention, the only one who has the capacity to define us and on whom our gaze is centered, then we can set healthy boundaries with everyone else.

When God is not in his rightful place, then we spend all our time trying to make everyone happy, or working at keeping everyone safe or pretending like no one else matters. Without God, all of these actions become destructive and will eventually cause pain and loss because they are all just expressions of the fear of man.

Chapter 37

As we close this story, you might be tempted to think that you are doing very well as you are and have avoided the pain of exposing your own heart.

That you have not bought all this religious mumbo jumbo about emotions, vulnerability and all the wrong, heart-related things I have been writing about.

I have to agree with you that this is one of the safest ways to get through this fallen and broken world, and, depending on how you define success, it is an effective way to succeed in it.

But there is just one more "small" problem you should also be aware of with this mentality. One day in the not too distant future, as a dust man, your body will return to dust and your heart will rise to meet the one who gave it life.

Then, everything you have avoided dealing with-- all the lies, deceit, jealousy, corruption, everything that you have guarded so well in that broken heart of yours--will be exposed for what it is. Because you see, when we walk into the presence of God, by the nature of his heart, he will expose all hearts for what they truly are, as nothing can hide in his presence.

Everything will be revealed for what it truly is. That is one of the laws of life that his Kingdom is built on. God is not trying to make life miserable here just for the fun of it. He is preparing us for this return to reality that is rushing towards us.

He is the only soil in which our hearts can truly grow and flourish, and if we will not prepare ourselves for it, we will spend eternity scratching out an existence in the soil of hell.

The choice is not really whether we will be vulnerable. The only real question is how.

Take the risk now, and grow up and discover what you have always wanted. Or be a coward and be exposed on that day for what you truly are.

The choice is yours.

About the Author

Matt Rawlins was born on the West Coast and grew up in a Christian home. He jokes that his earliest prayer was "Lord, help me not to swear." It seemed clear to him that if you didn't swear, you were a good person and if you were a good person, you could avoid hell and go to heaven. After all, wasn't that the purpose of heaven? To avoid hell?

In his late teens God began to stir his mind and he remembers sitting with his family around a dinner table and asking, "What is love?" It seems that question led him in desperation to find out if there was a real source of love or if the world was just a bad dream.

It was through this searching that Matt ended up doing a training program with Youth With A Mission (YWAM). He recalls, "One time when I was crying before God, words came to me that seemed to sum up my whole life. The words were 'I'm so lonely, I'm so lonely.' It was then that I realized Christianity was a relationship of love and not fear. I guess it was then that I realized how much Jesus loved me and I fell in love with him."

He volunteered with YWAM and spent three years working in Saipan, Micronesia. From there, he went on to Hong Kong where he met his beautiful wife, Celia, (she is from Hawaii). From Hong Kong they moved to Singapore to lead the YWAM work there. Their son, Joshua was born there. They were in Singapore for five years.

Later they moved to Oregon where Matt's family was living, and Matt went back to school. He finished his BA in Management and Communications and his Doctorate in leadership development and communication.

Currently the Rawlins family lives in Singapore where Matt does consulting and leadership training with businesses and churches. He can be contacted at:

Email: mrawlins@mac.com

Facebook: Matt Rawlins: Personal page
(If you see a young man with dreads with the same name, it is my neiphew. I am the old guy looking at the mountains.)
             Guardian: This book
             Green Bench Consulting: Company work

Consulting Business: thegreenbench.com

Other books by Matt Rawlins

Market Place Books

The Green Bench: A dialogue about leadership and change

      The book is a story between an old retired teacher who has taught children all his life and a young manager who has somehow survived the educational system, but still doesn't know how to learn. They meet by accident on a green park bench and a relationship begins that will change both of them.

      The old teacher, takes basic principles from his many years of teaching and weaves them through stories from his students who learned to learn. The young manager, blinded by the apparent complexity of the office world, sees that it is possible to learn and manage in the midst of chaos.

The Green Bench II: More dialogue about leadership & communication

      Join in as a friendship continues between a retired teacher and a young executive who is overwhelmed by the dilemmas he faces everyday.

Their dialogue explores questions like: Is there always a right way to do things? How do you deal with dilemmas? Why is there always tension? People think differently, how can we get along? How can I talk about difficult or even painful issues? How can I get the best information from those who have it but are afraid to give it to me?

The Lottery: A question can change a life

How do people succeed? Simply put, they know how to ask the right questions.

Relationships and businesses flourish when people know how to ask the right questions. Although it sounds simple enough, few of us have been taught the fine art of asking questions.

A better question uncovers a better answer. And, the right questions will release creativity, open the door to discovery and bring clarity to challenges.

There's an Elephant in the Room: Discover the Single Most Powerful Tool for Growth

What would happen if you had an elephant in your team or organization? Its presence is felt by all, yet no one is willing to talk about it?

The trouble is if you can't talk about something, you can't change it. If you can't change something, you miss out on new opportunities, creativity, achievements and success.

Explore through this engaging story, with its insightful illustrations, what happens to an organization when its people are silenced and elephants are free to roam wherever they want.

But then what would happen if you talked about the secrets everyone knows?

Discover what happens when 4 misfits in a dying company choose the courage to be honest with each other.

Books for the Church

Rediscovering Reverence: The path to intimacy

Are you aching for an intimate walk with God? One where you know He understands you and what you are going through? Where you understand His heart and desire for you, and you see His plan unfolding in your life? Rediscovering Reverence unlocks the mystery of walking in daily intimacy with God.

Many people understand and long for intimacy with God, but few realize that the fear of the Lord is a foundation for that. You can't have intimacy without reverence. This fast-paced and readable book maintains a compassionate and personable tone while challenging the reader spiritually and intellectually. Every Christian who yearns to discard his discontented, lukewarm lifestyle and pursue a serious and fulfilling life in God should read Rediscovering Reverence.

The Question: Is God good to all?

How would you feel if everyone you loved and everything you owned were destroyed in the twinkling of an eye? Would it alter your view of God?

Knowing the character of God will determine how you answer The Question. Satan was the first moral being to raise The Question. It goes to the very heart of God's kingdom: Is God good? To everyone? All the time? Through the life of a man called Job, The Question raises the ultimate test. How did Job respond when his world collapsed? What was his test?

The Namer: How do I find my true identity?

What would happen if you could change your name or your identity any time you wanted? What would be the consequences? This story explores the lives of King Saul and King David and how they wrestled with their identities. Although they had similar callings one turned away from God and the other walked intimately with God. One tried to name himself while the other accepted God's name for him. The name they accepted for themselves defined their relationship with God.

The Container: What holds the presence of God?

When a young man is nearly killed in a serious car accident, he raises questions about the meaning of life. His openness provides an opportunity for an intimate daily dialogue about all his relationships – his wife, his family, his co-workers, and finally, God.

Listen in as the young man and his father share their hearts and try to understand God's heart for each of us. If you have ever wondered why you can't make it on your own, why you are strongest when you acknowledge you are weak and why God created us to be interdependent on one another, you must read "The Container."

Emails from Hell: Evil schemes to undermine a leader

In this takeoff of C. S. Lewis' The Screwtape Letters, learn the devious ideas and strategies used to bring down leaders of groups, organizations — even nations — as you follow the diabolical email directives from an executive demon to his student trainee.

Mysteries Beyond the Gate & Other Peculiar Short Stories

Expect the unexpected in Mysteries Beyond The Gate & other peculiar short stories. Life is not always what it seems as you'll soon discover. These stories reveal that sometimes down is up, black is white and truth may be hidden in folly.

Through the delightful art of storytelling, author Matt Rawlins reveals delicious nuggets of truth that you will savor long after you finish reading. Some tales will defy your reality. Others will alter how you see the world around you. But each one will challenge your thinking!

These books may be purchased online as ebooks for $5.99. They can be found at:

mrawlinsonline.com

They may also be purchased through traditional books stores or at stores on the internet.

1 Gen 3:1-5
2 Gen 20:9
3 Isaiah 5:4
4 Jer 2:5
5 2 Thess 2:8
6 This paragraph was adapted from a paragraph in Gene Edwards, *Tale of Three Kings*,
7 This is an adapted quote from C.S. Lewis
8 Job 1:21
9 Job 2:10
10 Rom 4:18
11 Gen 17:17
12 Gen 22:2
13 Gen 22:12
14 The four values are adapted from the work of Dr. Chris Argyris. I studied these values for my graduate work and found them in everyone I studied regardless of age, culture, personality or gender.
15 The five areas here are adapted from the work of Patrick Lencioni and his book *Overcoming The Five Dysfunctions of a Team*.
16 Some ideas and this list of emotions are adapted from (1986) *The Emotional Hostage, Rescuing Your Emotional Life*, Cameron-Bandler, Leslie & Lebeau, Michael.
17 Hos 11:8
18 Zeph 3:17
19 Rev 6:15-17
20 Luke 6:7
21 John 5
22 Matt 23:33
23 Matt 15:14
24 Matt 23:13
25 Matt 23:25-6
26 Mark 7:6-7